FEYI FAY #1

AND THE CASE OF THE MYSTERIOUS
Madam Koi Koi

BY SIMISAYO BROWNSTONE

A TENI AND TAYO CREATIONS LLC BOOK

D1157261

For Teni and Tayo.
My Inspiration.

Feyi Fay
And The Case Of The Mysterious Madam Koi Koi
Text Copyright © 2018 Simisayo Brownstone
Illustrations Copyright © 2018 Teni and Tayo Creations LLC

First edition, July 2018
Summary: A magical adventure ensues when Feyi Fay is called to London to help a boy who believes on old Nigerian legend has come to life in his living room.

ISBN paperback: 978-1-7322315-0-4
ISBN eBook: 978-1-7322315-1-1

This book is published by Teni and Tayo Creation LLC.
For information about distribution or bulk purchases email:

contact@teniandtayo.com

Table of Contents

Chapter 1

The Kuzoolies are Coming!

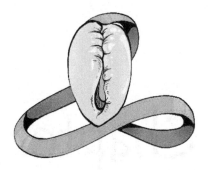

Beep Beep! Feyi's phone lights up. A child somewhere in the world needs her help. Feyi is a magical helper, called a Kuzooly, that helps kids whenever they are in need. She helps if they have a task to complete or a problem to solve. And if they are just looking for a little magic and adventure, she helps with that too.

Kuzoolies are magical creatures that look just like regular human beings, except they have wings. One could even say they look like fairies, but they are human-sized. And they don't live on the ground like you and me – they live on floating islands behind the clouds.

For many years, Kuzoolies watched humans from their islands behind the clouds. They wanted to visit and say hello but thought the humans would be afraid of them, so they remained in the sky. Quietly observing. Until one day, a young and adventurous Kuzooly, named Toyosi, snuck away, flew down to earth and introduced herself to a human child who had run away from home. The child was not afraid, the story goes. Toyosi and the girl developed a close friendship and she was able to convince her to return home. And after the child went home, Toyosi watched over her, making sure she was safe and happy.

It was through Toyosi's experience with this child that the Kuzoolies learned that only children could see them, and that the children could only see Kuzoolies who were not yet adults.

Toyosi was sad when she went to visit the girl years later but could not talk to her. Because Toyosi had grown up, the girl could no longer see her.

—

The elder Kuzoolies were angry with Toyosi for sneaking away and showing herself to humans, but at the same time, they were grateful. They learned that they had the power to help, and because of what Toyosi did, they decided that they would assist children around the world whenever they had a problem they could not solve on their own.

Toyosi later dedicated her life to learning about Kuzooly magic. She created lots of magical objects that children could use to contact Kuzoolies whenever they were in need and that the young Kuzoolies could use in situations when they needed a little help.

Many years passed by and Toyosi became an elder herself, and the keeper of all Kuzooly magic.

Chapter 2

A Call for Help

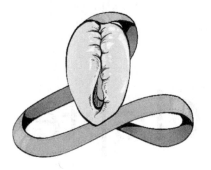

Feyi picks up her phone. There's a message in her magic Kuzooly app that says a child in London, England needs her.

If you want to contact a Kuzooly like Feyi for help, there are a few ways to do it. You can use the magic Kuzooly app that's hidden on every phone. Only children have the ability to see it. You can also dial a phone number and speak to a Kuzooly helper that only children can hear. Or you can send an email to an address only children know. You can even write a letter in ink that's invisible to adults. And if you can't find a phone, computer, or ink, then you can close your eyes real tight and hum a secret Kuzooly tune. A tune that kids learn from a giant Kuzooly called old man Uche. Then, maybe, just maybe, a Kuzooly will hear you and come fluttering down.

—

Now that Feyi has received a message calling for help, she needs to be in London in five minutes. Time works differently where Kuzoolies live. Five minutes to a Kuzooly is like one second to a child.

"Yay! I'm going to England," Feyi says to her best friend Kemi who is sitting next to her on a bench underneath a large oak tree. Feyi and Kemi are from different Kuzooly villages, but they always find time to get together under the oak tree and talk.

"I love England," Kemi says. She had been to London a few times before to help some children and had lots of fun adventures while she was there.

"The weather is so unpredictable," Kemi continues. "Is it hot? Is it cold? Is it raining or is it hailing? It's like being blindfolded at an ice cream store and trying to grab a scoop. Which flavor will you get? I love it!"

"Gosh! You are so weird," Feyi says, giggling. "I like it hot and sticky and icky, like a warm melted chocolate bath."

"Eww! You are weirder than I am!" Kemi exclaims. "Maybe that's why we are friends."

"Maybe that's why," Feyi says as she wraps her arm around Kemi's shoulders and giggles.

"I bet you it rains while you are in London," Kemi says with a smile.

Feyi and Kemi love to make bets with each other. It started one day when Feyi bet with Kemi that she'd beat her in a flying race. Kemi lost and had to do Feyi's laundry for a week.

Ever since then, they'd place bets with each other whenever they were unsure of something. Just for the fun of it. And whoever won the bet was always excited to pick a task that the other one had to do.

"I bet you it doesn't," Feyi responds confidently, even though she has no clue what the weather will be like. "Hmm, I've got to think about what I want you to do for me when I win," she giggles.

"Not going to happen!" Kemi exclaims.

"Ha! We'll see about that. Anyway, I have to go now. I'll tell you all about it when I get back."

"Okay, have fun in rainy London," Kemi chuckles.

Feyi looks at her phone again. She searches for the big red button in the magic Kuzooly app. The button allows her to magically disappear and reappear at the location shown in the app. She clicks the button and *poof.* She is gone.

Chapter 3

Madam Who?

Feyi arrives at the home of the child who called for help. But she arrives upside down in a laundry basket full of dirty clothes. "Not again!" she mutters. Sometimes the magic Kuzooly app is not very accurate and takes her to unexpected places.

In the past, she has mistakenly arrived on the wing of an airplane while it was still

in the air. She has also found herself in the
belly of a garbage truck filled with rotten

food and slippery banana peels. One time

she even landed splat on the back of an elephant during a circus show.

Feyi climbs out of the laundry basket, pulls three dirty socks off her head and looks around. She's in someone's bedroom. She sees a little boy, about 6 years old, sitting on the bed. He has messy blond hair and is wearing teddy bear pajamas. His eyebrows are high, and his mouth is wide open like he has just seen something really cool.

"Hello there," Feyi says. "I don't always make an entrance this way. The magic Kuzooly app misbehaves sometimes."

The boy doesn't say a word. What does one say to a Kuzooly that just came out of your laundry basket?

"My name is Feyi Fay," Feyi continues. "But you can call me Feyi. It's kind of like saying the word fairy but without the 'r.' What's your name?"

"My name is Tom," the boy replies slowly as he stares at Feyi. Her wings are big and blue. Her skin is the color of chocolate and her eyes are large and deep coffee brown. She's wearing her hair braided in two buns on the top of her head, but a few braids fall down the side of her face with red and gold beads dangling on the ends. She's also got an oddly shaped shell hanging down the middle of her forehead. It has a special purpose, but she'll tell Tom about that later. When the time is right.

"So nice to meet you, Tom." Feyi reaches out to shake his hand. She smiles wide from ear to ear. "How can I help you today?"

Tom frowns and makes crinkles on his forehead. "My friend, Tunde, told me about a woman who comes to take kids away if they open their eyes in the middle of the night after going to sleep. And when she walks she makes the sound – koi koi koi – on the floor. They call her Madam Koi Koi."

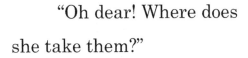

"Oh dear! Where does she take them?"

"To a place with no fun or ice cream," Tom replies with a quiver in his voice.

"The horror!" Feyi gasps with both hands pressed against her cheeks.

"Now, I can't sleep," Tom continues. "I just heard – koi koi koi – coming from the living room. I think Madam Koi Koi is talking to my mom and they are plotting to take away my ice cream... forever!"

Chapter 4

Oh, So Brave

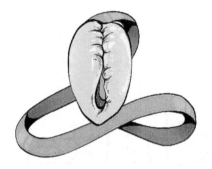

"Never ever!" Feyi pronounces with confidence. "That's why you have me," she says. "But is Madam Koi Koi really here? Now?"

"Yes! Let me show you." Tom jumps off the bed, runs to the bedroom door and peeks under it. He waves for Feyi to come over. Through the crack under the door they see the legs of a woman in red high heeled

shoes, but they can't see her face. And when

she moves her feet, the sound of her heels on

the wooden floor make the sound –

Koi Koi Koi

"Interesting," Feyi says.

They hear another sound, so they look under the door again. This time they see Tom's mom's legs walking out of the room towards the kitchen.

"I've got an idea," Feyi exclaims, jumping up. "We should go to the kitchen and ask your mom what she's up to."

"What?" Tom says, scratching his head in confusion. "But we know what she's up to! She doesn't want me to have any more ice cream. I think we should hide or run away so Madam Koi Koi doesn't get me."

"Never ever!" Feyi exclaims. "We can't run from our problems. Besides, she's your mom isn't she? I'm sure there is just a misunderstanding."

"But... but I'm scared Madam Koi Koi will get me," Tom says.

"I get scared sometimes too," Feyi replies. "Did you know I'm the only Kuzooly with blue wings? No one knows why. Sometimes the other Kuzoolies make fun of me and sometimes it makes me scared to make new friends."

"That's terrible. What do you do?" Tom asks with a sad look on his face.

"It's hard, but I try very hard to be brave," Feyi says. "There is an old saying my mom sometimes tells me that goes like this – *A gazelle that stays hidden and does not graze will starve.*"

"Huh? What?" Tom asks as if she had just spoken some sort of ancient foreign language. "I don't get it."

Feyi giggles. "It means that if you don't take the risk you will not get the reward."

Tom scratches his head. "I still don't get it," he says.

"Think about it like this. If the gazelle is not brave enough to go and graze, it means it will not eat and so it will starve. If I'm not brave enough to talk to people, I won't make any new friends. And if you are not brave enough to leave this room, you will not know what your mom is really up to. Sometimes, you have to muster up the courage to do something even if you are scared. Do you get it now?"

"Yes. Yes, I do," Tom replies.

"But!" Feyi continues, as her eyes light up. She grabs Tom by his shoulders and flashes a wide smile across her face. "The most fun thing I do when I'm scared is the *make me brave* pose, and then I feel even better. You should try it."

"The *make me brave* pose? What's that?" Tom asks, intrigued.

"I'll show you." Feyi waves her hand for Tom to stand up. "Ball your fists up and put them on your hips like this. Place your feet apart. Stick your chest out and say these words: *shavey cravey make me bravey*."

Tom chuckles. The words sound funny
to him. "Okay," he says. He does the pose

and says the words, *shavey cravey make me bravey*.

Feyi giggles. "Great job," she says. "Feel better now?"

"A little," Tom replies.

"Well, a little bit of something is better than a little bit of nothing," Feyi says, her wings fluttering happily. "Now let's do this!"

Chapter 5

Glitter Everywhere

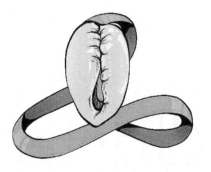

Tom smiles. "Alright, let's do it!" he
says boldly with his fists on his hips and his
chest puffed out. "But wait! How do we get
to the kitchen without Madam Koi Koi
seeing us?"

"That's what my magic cowry bead is
for," Feyi says, pointing to the oddly shaped
shell hanging down the middle of her
forehead.

All Kuzoolies have a cowry bead that gives them magical powers. But young Kuzoolies like Feyi can only access a small portion of the bead's powers. They can only use the cowry bead to call magical objects that were created by Elder Toyosi. And, they can't decide which object they get. The cowry bead senses what the problem is and sends the best magical object for the job. That all changes when Kuzoolies becomes adults, because then they are able to tap into the full power of the cowry bead and practice great magic.

Feyi closes her eyes and says the magic words –

Cham Cham
Cheeky Cheeky
Yaa!

As she says the words the bead on her forehead glows bright, like a burning yellow sun. Tom takes a few steps back as Feyi does her magic. Suddenly, a piece of cardboard covered in glitter appears in Feyi's hands. *Pop!*

Tom looks at it, his head tilted to one side and his lips pursed like a duck's.

Feyi sees that Tom is confused. "It's a *glitter me invisible board!*" she exclaims. "If you stand behind it, the shimmering glitter makes you invisible.

"Ooh," Tom says with wide eyes. He's impressed by the invisibility. He's not so sure about all that glitter.

"We can use it to sneak past Madam Koi Koi and get to the kitchen."

Feyi shakes the cardboard to sprinkle a little glitter all over them. Then the cardboard starts to get bigger and bigger. Big enough for both of them to hide behind. They get behind the cardboard, open the bedroom door and tiptoe past Madam Koi Koi towards the kitchen. With each step they take a little more glitter sprinkles all over them. Feyi loves the glitter. Tom does not.

"Ugh," Tom groans.

"Shh," Feyi says with her index finger pressed against her lips. "Madam Koi Koi can't see us, but she can certainly hear us."

But it's too late. Madam Koi Koi has heard something. She stands up and walks towards them – koi koi koi – the sound of her shoes on the floor.

Feyi and Tom stand very still and very quiet. Madam Koi Koi looks around. She stares directly at the spot where they are standing but doesn't see anything. Feyi and Tom stay quiet, and frozen like statues. Madam Koi Koi waits a little, but still doesn't see or hear anything, so she walks away.

"Phew," they say together. Quietly.

"That was close," Tom whispers. Then they continue to tiptoe to the kitchen. But by the time they get there, Tom's mom is gone.

"Where did she go?" Tom asks, dusting the glitter off his pajamas. He spins around and around, as he tries to reach the glitter on his back. He looks like a silly dog chasing its tail.

Feyi giggles. "I don't know," she replies, as she helps Tom brush the glitter off his back. Then she brushes a little off herself, too.

Suddenly, they hear footsteps again –

Koi Koi Koi

This time it's coming towards the kitchen.

"It's Madam Koi Koi. Quick! Hide!" Tom whispers frantically. He grabs Feyi's hand and pulls her into the kitchen pantry.

He shuts the door behind them. They peek under the pantry door and see Madam Koi Koi's legs in red high heeled shoes. They still can't see her face. She walks to the refrigerator, grabs something and then walks out.

"Phew!" They both sigh.

Chapter 6

Little Ants

"Let's go back to my room. We need a
new plan," Tom says. He tries to open the
pantry door, but it won't budge. He tries
again. It still won't open. "Oh no! We're
stuck."

"Never ever!" Feyi exclaims. "Not while
I'm here." She closes her eyes and says the
magic words.

Cham Cham Cheeky Cheeky Yaa!

The cowry bead glows. Then suddenly, a short wooden stick appears. Pop!

Tom looks at the stick, scrunching his nose. It doesn't look like it can do much.

"It's a *shake me shrink me stick*," Feyi explains. "You shake it and you shrink."

"You have such weird names for everything," Tom laughs.

"I wasn't the one that gave them names," Feyi responds. "There is a Kuzooly we call Elder Toyosi who creates and names all the magical objects. She's a little kooky," Feyi giggles.

Tom giggles too. "Okay, let's give it a try," he says.

First, Feyi shakes the stick a few times and then Tom shakes it. Then they slowly

shrink and become so small they can fit underneath the pantry door. Like little ants.

"Awesome!" Tom says in awe as he looks around. Feyi watches Tom observe his surroundings. Everything looks so big. The chairs look like mountains. The white ceiling looks like it's a giant cloud way up in the sky. It reminds Feyi of what her home looks like to humans when they stare up at it from the ground.

Even though Kuzooly islands are in the sky behind the clouds, they have dense forests and wide-open spaces. Each Kuzooly family lives in a treehouse with colorful patterns on the walls that are unique to each family. All except for one Kuzooly – Old man Uche. Old man Uche is a giant grumpy Kuzooly that lives on a cloud all by himself.

At night on the Kuzooly islands, the leaves on the trees glow like little lanterns hanging from the branches. Neither adults nor children can see the Kuzooly islands floating in the sky. When they look up at the sky, all they see are clouds.

Chapter 7

Cookie! Cookie!

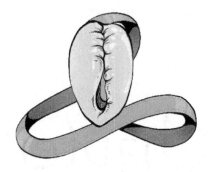

Back in the pantry, Tom and Feyi are still as tiny as ants. They look around. In the distance, Tom sees a breadcrumb from a sandwich he had eaten earlier. It looks like a large soccer ball. He runs towards it and kicks it. He forgets that sometimes where there are crumbs, there are ants. Suddenly, he turns around and sees a giant ant, the size of a lion, walking towards them. It's snapping its mandibles and waving its antennae.

"Aargh!" Tom screams. He grabs Feyi's hand and they run as far away from the giant ant as they can. "I don't want to be small anymore. Say the magic *gimme gimme* words!" he screams again.

Feyi giggles. "Okay, okay. Relax," she says in a calming voice. "Let's see what object the cowry bead will give us this time." She closes her eyes and says the words —

Cham Cham
Cheeky Cheeky
Yaa!

Pop! A chocolate chip cookie appears.

Tom looks at it with a smile on his face. He doesn't know what it does, but anything with chocolate chips in it can only be a good thing.

"It's a *fatten me up cookie*. 100% organic, of course," Feyi says with a smile.

She gives the cookie to Tom. "Eat it," she says.

Tom scarfs down the cookie as fast as he can. But he only grows a little.

"Uh oh," Feyi says. "Because we are so small, the cookie is also small and doesn't have full power. We need a whole lot more of those cookies."

"Huh?" Tom says.

"We have to say the magic words over and over and over again, until we get a lot of cookies," she says. "Then we have to eat them all!"

"We have to eat them all?" Tom can't help but be happy about that. His mom never allows him to have cookies or dessert before bedtime. "Let's do it," he says with a big grin on his face.

Feyi giggles. "Let's! Say the words with me."

Cham Cham
Cheeky Cheeky
Yaa!

Feyi and Tom say the words together. Pop! A cookie appears and plops down on the floor. Tom picks it up and eats it.

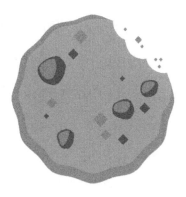

"Cham-Cham Cheeky-Cheeky Yaa," they say again. Pop! Another cookie appears. Feyi eats it.

"Cham Cham Cheeky Cheeky Yaa." Pop! Another cookie. Tom eats it.

They say the words over and over and they each eat the cookies until they are almost full size again.

As Tom is eating the last bite, his mom walks back into the kitchen. "You're eating food off the floor?" she gasps. "That's nasty!"

"Yes! That's nasty, Tom." Feyi giggles. Tom's mom can't see or hear her.

Tom smiles coyly. "Oopsy," he says.

Chapter 8

The Big Reveal

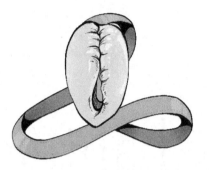

"Ask her! Ask her the question." Feyi exclaims as she pokes Tom gently on his lower back.

"Okay, okay," he says under his breath, and then he asks. "Mommy, why are you plotting with Madam Koi Koi to take away my fun and ice cream?"

"Madam Koi Koi?" his mom asks, with a wrinkle on her forehead. "Who is that?"

"The woman who is in the living room with you. The one with the red shoes."

"You mean your aunt Jessica?"

"Auntie Jessica?" Tom says. "That's who's in the living room?" His jaw almost drops to the floor.

He runs to the living room and peeks in. And sure enough, he sees his aunt Jessica sitting on the sofa in her red high heeled shoes. He slaps his hand on his forehead.

Aunt Jessica had come to visit Tom's mom on her way home from work to discuss an important matter. Nothing related to fun or ice cream. Tom can't believe that he thought she was Madam Koi Koi this whole time.

"Is that my favorite nephew over there?" Aunt Jessica says when she notices Tom peeking into the living room. "Come here and give me a squeeze."

Tom hesitates for a moment, then he walks over to his aunt and gives her a hug.

"Shouldn't you be in bed by now," aunt Jessica asks.

"Yes auntie," Tom replies slowly. He looks down at the ground as if he is embarrassed. "But I couldn't sleep."

"Bad dreams?"

"Ummm." Tom mumbles. He isn't sure how to answer the question.

Just then, Tom's mom walks back into the living room. "It's getting late, Tom, honey," she says. "Give your aunt kisses and say goodnight."

"Okay. Goodnight auntie," Tom says and then gives his aunt a kiss on the cheek.

"Goodnight," she replies. "Try to get some sleep, okay?"

"I will."

Tom's mom reaches out to hold Tom's hand. "Come with me sweetheart. Let's go to bed," she says. Then they both walk to Tom's bedroom together, hand in hand.

—

"So, sweetie, tell me about this Madam Koi Koi," Tom's mom says once they get back to Tom's bedroom.

Tom tells her the story about the woman that comes to take kids away in the night and makes the sound – koi koi koi – when she walks.

"Sounds terrible," Tom's mom says. "But honey, that sounds like just a story that some parents tell their kids to make sure they stay asleep at night. It's not real. And even if it was, remember that I am always here to protect you. No madam is taking you away from me. No sir. Not on my watch. I'm a fierce mama, grrrr," she growls

with a snarly look on her face.

Tom chuckles.

"Now, it's late and you really need to be in bed," Tom's mom says. "I'll put a picture of me beside your bed so that if you wake up at night you see my face and remember that I am always here to protect you."

"Okay mom," Tom says, feeling better, but also a little silly. She gives him a hug, kisses him goodnight and tucks him into bed.

After Tom's mom leaves, Feyi does a flip in the air and lands on Tom's bed. She had been quietly watching everything unfold. "Looks like my job here is done," she says with in a cheerful tone in her voice, a happy look on her face and her arms stretched out wide.

Tom jumps out of bed and gives her a big hug. "This was SO much fun!"

"Aww, I had fun too," Feyi says, happy that she was able to help.

Tom gets back into his bed and lays his head on his pillow, ready for sleep. It has been an exhausting evening. "Do you have to go?" he asks, yawning. But before Feyi can respond, Tom falls fast asleep and begins to snore.

Feyi giggles. "Goodbye," she whispers. "Sleep well."

—

Now, it's time to see more of London, Feyi thinks. She always takes the time to explore whatever city she is in before she has to go home. She brings out her phone, opens the magic Kuzooly app and sets the destination for Big Ben. She clicks the big red button in the app and *poof*. She is gone.

Chapter 9

London Calling

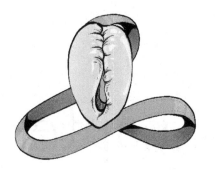

Feyi sits at the top of Big Ben looking out. Big Ben is a giant clock that stands in the heart of London. The sky is clear, there's a full moon and the air is crisp. She wraps her wings around her body as she watches the glowing city. Little cars and large red double decker buses bustle down the narrow roads.

The London Eye Ferris wheel spins lazily around and around. Cruise boats on the

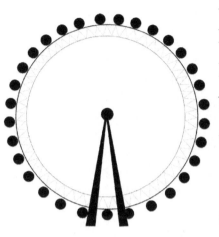 River Thames sail leisurely by. London is so beautiful, she thinks.

Suddenly, she feels a raindrop on her cheek. Then another and another and another.

"It's raining? How can that be! The sky was clear just a moment ago," she says out loud. She waves her fists in the air in frustration as raindrops slide down her arms. Her best friend, Kemi, was right. The weather in London is very unpredictable.

Suddenly, she remembers the bet that
she made with Kemi before she came to
London. Kemi had bet with her that it would

rain. Now she realizes that Kemi was right about that too. "Oh no!" she says. "I wonder what Kemi will want me to do for her."

Feyi opens the magic Kuzooly app on her phone and sets the destination for home. She clicks the red button and *poof*. She's in her bedroom, in her colorful treehouse, in a dense forest, on a floating island behind the clouds.

Chapter 10

Chores or Snacks?

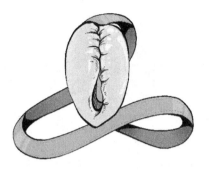

The next day, Feyi and her best friend, Kemi, are sitting on the bench under their usual oak tree, catching up.

"How was London?" Kemi asks. She is wearing her hair puffy like cotton candy and just like Feyi, she has a cowry bead dangling down the middle of her forehead. But unlike Feyi, her wings are purple.

"It was fun," Feyi replies. "I met a little
boy who couldn't sleep because he thought
there was a woman in his living room
coming to take him away. He thought she

was coming to take him to a place with no fun. We couldn't believe it was just his aunt. She had come to visit his mom." Feyi giggles.

"That's funny. What an adventure!" Kemi says.

"How about you?" Feyi asks. "Did you get to help any kids while I was gone?"

"Yes," Kemi replies. "I went to India to help a girl who accidentally broke her mom's favorite vase. She was scared to tell her mom the truth because she knew she would be really mad. But we knew she had to tell the truth. It all worked out okay in the end. Phew!"

"Nice! Honesty is the best policy my mom always says."

"So, I have an important question," Kemi says, looking at Feyi with her lips slightly curled upwards. "Did it rain while you were in London?"

"Ugh! Yes, it did." Feyi sighs. "You won the bet."

"Hurray!" Kemi exclaims as she wiggles on the bench and flaps her big purple wings.

"So, what do I owe you?"

Kemi takes off her shoes and plops her bare feet on Feyi's lap. "My feet hurt. I need a nice long foot massage."

"Eeew," Feyi says, scrunching her nose. "Smelly feet."

Kemi wiggles her toes on Feyi's lap.

"Go on. My feet are waiting," she sings.

Feyi begins to massage Kemi's feet, still scrunching her nose. She doesn't like to lose bets, so she comes up with another one while she is massaging Kemi's feet. "I bet you that the next child that calls for my help will be in a country that's hot," she says.

"Hmmm," Kemi says, thinking about whether she wants to take the bet. "Okay," she says finally. "I bet you that it will be cold and rainy."

"Yay! I'm so happy you took the bet because I already know exactly what I want when I win," Feyi says, rubbing her palms together cheerfully.

"So do I!" Kemi exclaims.

"Okay, you go first then."

"Okay. Remember how you promised to go with me to visit old man Uche?"

"Yes." Feyi shudders. "He can be so mean sometimes."

Old man Uche, the giant grumpy Kuzooly that lives on a cloud all by himself, spends his days sitting on his cloud and humming a tune that only Kuzoolies and children can hear. Kuzoolies love the sound of the tune that old man Uche hums. They even like it when children hum the tune. And if they happen to hear a child humming the tune as they are passing by, they will swoop down quickly to be near him or her. Sometimes, the smaller Kuzoolies go to visit old man Uche on his cloud so that they can hear the tune more clearly. But whenever they get too close to him, it makes him upset and he yells so loud that his voice hurts their ears and his breath turns into a strong wind that blows them all away. Even

humans on the ground can hear it when old man Uche yells, but to them, it sounds like thunder.

"He's not so bad," Kemi says. "He's only mean if you get too close. We won't get too close. And I heard that he is nice if you take him some akara to eat."

Akara is a snack that Kuzoolies often eat. It is made of black-eyed beans and shaped like little balls. Feyi had never met a Kuzooly who didn't love it.

"And WHEN I win the bet," Kemi continues, "You have to make a basket of akara for old man Uche before we go," she says, grinning.

"Oh no!" Feyi gasps, slapping her hand on her forehead. She loves to eat akara but she sure does not like to make them. The ingredients take such a long time to prepare. She has to get the beans, wash the beans, peel the beans, blend the beans and the list goes on. It can take hours to get the akara ready. But, whenever Feyi does takes the time to make them, many Kuzoolies say it is the best akara they have ever tasted. "Okay, deal. I'll make the akara IF you win," she says.

"Yay! I'm so excited. I can't wait to eat your akara and listen to old man Uche humming his tune," Kemi says, flapping her wings and clapping her hands together in excitement.

"Don't get too excited yet. Listen to what I want when *I* win," Feyi says.

"Okay. I'm listening," Kemi says.

"I know you must have heard that Elder Toyosi has created something special. A magic object that can do magic that no Kuzooly has ever seen before."

Elder Toyosi rarely creates new magical objects. But when she does, it is a cause for celebration.

"Yes. Go on," Kemi says, leaning forward a little.

"Well, as you know, Elder Toyosi is going to reveal this magical object to all Kuzoolies next week." Feyi continues. "Kuzoolies from all the surrounding villages and clouds will gather on a special night to learn about this new object and what it does."

"Yes, yes, I know," Kemi says, bouncing up and down on the bench, impatiently. "What has all this got to do with what you want me to do for you?"

Feyi giggles. "My mom won't let me go until I've done my chores."

"Ah ha!" Kemi rolls her eyes and sighs.

"You guessed it. I need you to do my chores so that I can go to Elder Toyosi's announcement," Feyi says as her wings flutter happily.

"Ugh. I hate chores," Kemi says. "But okay. I'll do it IF you win."

"Haha! Don't worry, it won't take long," Feyi says, as she flaps her wings and whips her hips from side to side doing a happy dance.

"You are way too happy for someone who is about to lose a bet. You'll soon be making a giant-sized basket of akara for old man Uche," Kemi chuckles.

"Haha! Let's see about that."

Feyi brings out her phone and drops it on the grass. Both girls lay down on the grass beside the phone and stare at it –

waiting for it to beep. Waiting to find out

where the next child that calls for help will be from. It could take minutes, hours, or days for another child to call for help. Each girl is eager to win the bet. So, they sit and wait. Feyi twirls her fingers around one of her braids, her heart thumping, while Kemi leans over the phone, eyes wide. Nearly thirty minutes pass by and Feyi is almost tired of staring at the screen. But then, suddenly, the phone sounds —beep beep! Kemi and Feyi shriek in excitement. They both lean in, bumping heads, as they eagerly look to see the location that has appeared in the magic Kuzooly app.

Who will win the bet? Find out in Feyi Fay Volume 2. Available now!

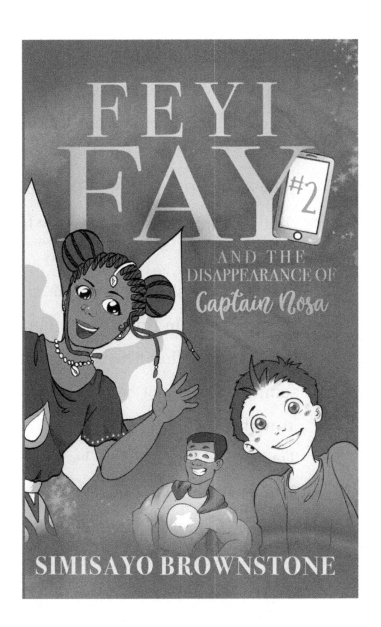

FEYI FAY #2

AND THE DISAPPEARANCE OF
Captain Nosa

SIMISAYO BROWNSTONE

Discussion Questions

1. If you could create a magical object, what would it be and what would it do?

2. Why do you think Tom didn't know that Madam Koi Koi was really his aunt Jessica?

3. Tom couldn't sleep because he thought Madam Koi Koi was in his living room. What are other reasons someone might not be able to sleep at night?

4. Tom's mom had a snarly look on her face when she told him she'd always be there to protect him. What does snarly mean? Show off your best snarly face.

5. What other ways could Tom have solved the problem without calling Feyi for help?

6. Feyi giggles a lot. Why do you think that is?

7. What was your favorite part of the book?

8. If you could call a Kuzooly for help, what problem would you want help with?

Crack the code to unlock a free, printable, Feyi Fay activity sheet

How many times does Feyi giggle in the story?

<u>45</u> <u>43</u> <u>65</u> <u>34</u> <u>81</u> <u>65</u>

=

_ _ _ _ _ _

Insert the cracked code in the URL below. With the help of a parent or guardian, visit the URL to unlock the Feyi Fay activity sheet.

feyifay.com/_ _ _ _ _ _

See the next page for the decoding sheet.

The Decoding Sheet

Use the letter/number key below to crack the code on the previous page.

A	46	K	11	U	99
B	32	L	34	V	81
C	21	M	77	W	43
D	27	N	72	X	57
E	65	O	20	Y	64
F	51	P	10	Z	86
G	58	Q	49		
H	60	R	78		
I	34	S	15		
J	22	T	45		

Join The Club!

Learn more about Feyi Fay, African culture and more. It's FREE.

www.feyifay.com/club

Stay in touch with Feyi Fay on social media. Follow us at
Instagram @feyifay & @teniandtayo

Facebook @feyifayadventures